By
Johanna Thydell

Illustrated by
Charlotte Ramel

There's a PIG in My Class!

Translated by
Helle Martens

Holiday House / New York

This is the loneliest pig in the world.
Behind him is the school.
Pig watches the children, smells their tasty snacks,
and hears the happy thud of their feet.

Something inside Pig
screams, "NOW."
He starts to dig . . .
and shovel.

He burrows
and furrows.

Suddenly, Pig is free.
He is scared, but his legs know
just where to take him.

A girl with honey-colored hair opens the gate quietly.
"*Shhhh!*" she warns as Pig sneaks in.

Although most of the children can't speak Pig's language,
they understand one another.

He wants to play, and in school, everyone has to be
included. That's the rule!

But pigs aren't allowed in school.
What should the children do?
Luckily, Honey Hair has an idea.
"Give Pig your sweater," she says.
"You give him your pants, and you give him a scarf."

"*Everyone inside!*" calls Tall Tina.
The children surround Pig and pretend
that nothing unusual is going on.
Their plan will never work.

Or will it?
"Ouch! Owww!" screams Honey Hair as loudly as she can.
Tall Tina rushes over, and suddenly Pig is inside!
He can hardly believe his own curly tail. He made it to school!

Pig feels a little left out during circle time.
He doesn't know the words to the songs.
But then he decides to sing along anyway.
Luckily, the children are singing so loudly that no one hears his grunts.

It's playtime! Finally!

The children play Toss the Ring on Pig's Snout and Pin the Tail on Pig, and crawl under his belly, pretending he is a bridge.

Their hair tickles Pig's skin, making him giggle so hard he blows bubbles out his snout.

At lunchtime there is no chair for Pig.
Honey Hair tells him to sit on the empty one next to her.
She tells him that one child is home sick today.
Pig feels sorry for One Child, but he's happy to have his
own place to sit with all his new friends.

It's hard to keep Pig a secret, but the other table manages
to make sure the teachers are busy.
"What is wrong with all of you today?" the teachers ask.

At naptime Honey Hair tells Pig what to do.
He can rest where One Child usually sleeps.
Pig still feels sorry for One Child, but only a little bit.

Pig hasn't had this much fun in ages.
His tummy is full, and he has friends galore.
Pig falls asleep happily snuggled up next to Honey Hair.

"Come on, Pig, get up, get up!" says Honey Hair.
She shows him how to wash in the bathroom.

Pig fills up the sink and splashes around.
He's thirsty. *Slurp, slurp, slosh!* Pig's sweater gets wet.
Water never tasted so good to Pig.

"Oh my," says Tall Tina to Pig. "You've made a pig out of yourself. You had better take off those wet clothes."
The children can't bear to look.

Tall Tina helps Pig get out of his wet things and cries,
"There's a pig in my class!"

Tall Tina grabs Pig's ears to drag him outside.
The children grab Pig's tail to keep him inside.
His curly tail becomes aaaaaall straight.

Everyone tugs and tugs and tugs.
But the children are too small.
They aren't strong enough, and suddenly . . .

. . . Pig is back outside.

"Good-bye, Pig!"

The children pet Pig for a long time through the fence until Tall Tina tells them to stop.

Then they pet Pig a little more as they wave good-bye.

   Pigs grunts in his own language about the wonderful time he has had and tells the children how much he'll miss them. The children all understand.

   So long, school. So long, children. So long, good times.

Here again is the loneliest pig in the world.

He misses the children and can't stop thinking about the fun he had with them.

He turns his back to the school and tries to pretend it isn't there.

But it's hard. Pig imagines he can hear the happy thuds of the children's feet again.

And no wonder! The children are on their way over to visit him! Take a look.

Eleven small snouts and two big ones enter the pigpen.
Brightly colored buckets of water chime like bells as the
children walk.

Tall Tina tells Pig she's sorry for being so harsh.
She explains that sometimes when you are
scared, you act before you think.

Pig understands. He is also scared sometimes—especially of being alone.
Tall Tina says that even though Pig cannot come to the school, the
school can come to him! Surely he has a lot to teach the children about
animals and nature.

Perhaps this is true. But right now Pig just wants
to play with the children for a long, long time.
He's very happy doing just that.

First published in Sweden as DET ÄR EN GRIS PÅ DAGIS in 2012 by Alfabeta Bokförlag, Stockholm
First published in the United States of America in 2014 by Holiday House, New York
English translation © 2014 by Holiday House, Inc.
Translated by Helle Martens
Printed and Bound in April 2014 at Tien Wah Press, Johor Bahru, Johor, Malaysia.
www.holidayhouse.com
First American Edition
1 3 5 7 9 10 8 6 4 2

Library of Congress Cataloging-in-Publication Data
Thydell, Johanna.
[Det är en gris på dagis. English]
There's a pig in my class! / by Johanna Thydell ; illustrated by Charlotte Ramel ; translated by Helle Martens. — First American edition.
pages cm
First published in Swedish as Det är en gris på dagis in 2012 by Alfabeta.
Summary: A lonely pig sneaks into school where he enjoys lunchtime and making new friends.
ISBN 978-0-8234-3168-7 (hardcover)
[1. Schools—Fiction. 2. Pigs—Fiction.] I. Ramel, Charlotte, illustrator. II. Martens, Helle, translator. III. Title. IV. Title: There is a pig in my class!
PZ7.T4313Th 2014
[E]—dc23
2013045492